How My Da
Taught Me to Dance

MW00955371

Susie Rich

How My Daddy Taught Me to Dance, Published August, 2014

Interior and Cover Illustrations: Randy Jennings
Interior Layout: Howard Johnson, Howard Communigrafix, Inc.
Editorial and Proofreading: Eden Rivers Editorial Services and Susan Herbert
Proofreading: Karen Grennan
Author Photo: Nelson Nieves Photography

Published by SDP Publishing an imprint of SDP Publishing Solutions, LLC.

For more information about this book contact Lisa Akoury-Ross by email at
lross@SDPPublising.com.

All rights reserved. No part of the material protected by this copyright notice may be reproduced or utilized in any form or by any means, electronic or mechanical, including photocopying, recording, or by any information storage and retrieval system, without written permission from the copyright owner.

To obtain permission(s) to use material from this work, please submit a written request to:

SDP Publishing
Permissions Department
PO Box 26, East Bridgewater, MA 02333
or email your request to info@SDPPublishing.com.

ISBN-13 (print): 978-0-9899723-1-4
ISBN-13 (ebook): 978-0-9899723-2-1

Library of Congress Control Number: 2013950941

Printed in the United States of America

Copyright © 2013, Susie Rich

ACKNOWLEDGMENTS

I would like to thank everyone who has supported my work: my publisher, Lisa Akoury-Ross, at SDP Publishing Solutions, LLC; my editors, Lisa Schleipfer at Eden Rivers Editorial and Susan Herbert; my illustrator, Randy Jennings; Howard Johnson at Howard Communigrafix, Inc.; and all those who have read, and will read, my stories.

I would like to dedicate this book to Burnette T. and Etta M. Burke, and to John R. and Edna M. Rich.

Jensine's head moved to the rhythm of the music as she listened to the sounds of each instrument.

"Pam pam pam pa pam a pam, ting ting, ba boom ba boom ba boom," went the drums as she watched her daddy's friend, "Wobble-Head" as they called him, beat with delight. Her eyes trailed off to the trumpet next. She loved its smooth, solid tones as the sound seemed to glide through the air, "Whee ow whee ow whee whee whee ow."

Mr. Jimmy was the trumpet player's name. He always seemed to close his eyelids as he played, but you could see his eyes, just under the lids, move to the sound of the music if you watched him closely enough. One could easily imagine what he felt as the music moved him with joy.

"Tat tat ta ti taa taa ti ta taaa." Her attention was suddenly grabbed by one of her favorite sounds, which was the piano.

Her shoulders jumped with joy, and her feet began to tap as she watched Keyoko move swiftly into her piano solo. Jensine moved closer to watch as Keyoko's fingers danced across the keys. Jensine looked on with amazement as every note came together perfectly.

Keyoko swayed from side to side, her head moving with the rhythm of the beat, her mouth opening, but no sound coming out. Jensine watched as Keyoko's long, jet-black hair tumbled in and out of her face, at times seeming to be dancing all on its own.

"Boom boom boom ba ba ba baaa." Jensine smiled as she heard the deep tone announcing the arrival of the bass solo. She turned to watch her daddy as his fingers climbed up and down the strings of the bass as if tickling it. The great upright bass appeared to laugh with pleasure as its deep sound filled the room. She loved to watch and listen as his pace quickened and his forehead creased. Almost instantly, he began the familiar licking and biting of his bottom lip.

She had asked him once if it hurt. "No," he said, and laughed. "I didn't even know I was doing it," he chuckled.

This was only one of a few of the expressions of the love for music she witnessed. She realized none of the musicians knew what funny faces they made while playing.

"After all, they have probably never watched themselves play," she giggled to herself.

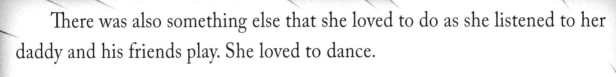

There was also something else that she loved to do as she listened to her daddy and his friends play. She loved to dance.

Jensine took her place on the floor and let the sounds of the jazz music move her as they had done a hundred times before. As she listened, she recalled the movements that she had learned at her dance class, and would choreograph her own performance piece while listening to Daddy's music.

Her daddy had taught her long ago how to let the music move her, and how to share her space with it. Respecting and understanding its different sounds and tones was like talking to many different people. He would say music had different shapes, sizes, colors, and moods that would move her in different ways.

At first she did not understand, but now she knew the music as her partner and her friend. It carried her with it beyond what the eye could see, but to where she could feel it.

Daddy's music often allowed her to try new things, and to use her imagination to the fullest. "The sudden changes in the rhythms are great for modern dance," she thought.

She also loved to hear him play gospel music. She always practiced her ballet piece while sitting in a church pew, even though she could only go over the steps in her head while the choir sang and the musicians played.

She loved imagining new ways to perform. She would close her eyes and just listen as the choir sang. After getting home from church, she would practice as soon as she possibly could. She could hardly wait to go over the choreography she had created while listening to the choir.

One day Jensine arrived at dance class, but to her surprise there was even more excitement than usual at the studio. All the children were gathered around the bulletin board laughing and chatting away. Before Jensine could squeeze her way to the front to see what held so much interest, her teacher, Ms. Amanda, appeared just inside the studio door.

"Children, calm down," she said with a smile. "Those of you who have class at this time go and begin your stretches." The children immediately went to their class.

"What was all that about?" Jensine whispered to her friend, Jessie, as they entered the studio.

"The audition!" said Jessie, her eyes sparkling with excitement. "I can't wait to find out more." She told Jensine all she had heard and knew about it.

As the class began, Ms. Amanda could see that her students could not wait to hear the announcements, which she usually made at the end of class. "Just this once," she said, seeing the eagerness of the children to find out more about the big audition, "I'll make the announcement before we begin."

"The audition you have seen posted on the board is for an open cast, meaning that the production company will look at a number of dancers because they produce several ballets. There are *The Nutcracker*, *Giselle*, and *Coppélia*, just to name a few," Ms. Amanda explained.

"If you want to participate, you must choreograph a finished piece in a little less than six weeks. I will be happy to help anyone who wants help; flyers will be passed out at the end of class."

"Does anyone have any questions?" Ms. Amanda asked, as several hands went up in the air. Jensine knew she should listen more closely to the questions, but she could only think about what piece she should do, what music she should use, and how she had only six weeks to choreograph the perfect performance.

"Last two questions," her teacher said before starting the class.

"Where will the auditions be held?" Jessie asked.

"The auditions will be held right here in the studio, and each performer will be given an instruction sheet and two minutes to perform his or her piece."

"Can we perform together?" asked another student.

"Yes," replied Ms. Amanda, "but each dancer will be judged on his or her individual performance."

"Now, no more questions. Let's start class," she said. "Get into your positions to stretch."

The class seemed to be over quickly, and all the children ran out to tell their parents about the big audition. Jensine could tell by the look on her mother's face that she already knew about what was going on. Jensine could see the parents were just as excited as the kids.

"Good-bye, Jessie!" Jensine called as she hurried out the door.

The next six weeks were full of fun for Jensine, as the whole family helped her with her routine. Her mother, her father, and her brother, Duane, gave her lots of support. The day of the audition came quickly, but Jensine was prepared.

As she arrived at the studio, her heart seemed to quicken just a bit as she saw some of her friends running up the front stairs.

"Oh my, oh my," she said as the car finally came to a stop.

"I know you are excited, but I know you will be wonderful," said Jensine's mother as she helped her out of the car. "Don't forget your music," she reminded Jensine, as she closed the car door. They walked hurriedly up to the studio.

When she walked into the studio, Jensine could not believe this was where she came for dance class three times a week. It was transformed into a professional studio and stage. There were big, bright lights, and Jensine counted at least three cameras.

"I will see you when you are done," said Jensine's mother, giving her a soft kiss on the forehead. "God bless," she added, as she disappeared into the studio.

"Attention! Attention, everyone!" A woman stood in the middle of the room. "My name is Ms. King; I am with the King Production Company. All parents are welcome to wait for your children quietly in the studio. After each child performs, he or she will be asked to leave. Any information we need concerning a student, we will obtain from the school's director."

All eyes turned to the dance director, Mrs. Eastman, as she smiled shyly. "You will not hear from us," Ms. King continued, "unless we are interested in your child. Thank you."

Jensine squeezed through the crowd as the parents began to leave. "Dancers, you will be given a number, and when your number is called please give your music to our music director and position yourself center stage to do your piece," Ms. King announced.

Jensine was handed a slip of paper with the number seventeen on it. She looked around at the other dancers and counted twenty-four altogether. She was glad because it gave her a chance to see most of the other performers.

All sat quietly and still as the auditions began. Most were solos, some were duets, but all were wonderful.

"Sixteen; number sixteen," the announcer bellowed.

"Sixteen already," Jensine thought. "That means I'm next." She picked up her music and moved toward the music station. She watched as the dancer ended his performance and moved quickly offstage.

"Seventeen; number seventeen," was announced just as Jensine reached the music station.

"Song number two," Jensine whispered, as she handed over the CD. She walked softly to center stage with her shoulders back and her neck stretched long. She closed her eyes, but only for a second, as the brief introduction began to play.

When she heard the bass, she thought about her daddy and imagined him playing to her right then. "Amazing Grace" was the song she had chosen, and a ballet piece was what she had arranged.

As the music seemed to seep into her movements, she heard her daddy's voice in the notes. "Let the music move you," it said as she glided across the stage.

Starting in fifth position, Jensine began her routine. She was a little nervous at first, but that rapidly faded as the music grew. She glided into an arabesque, then a waltz, and continued with several impressive leaps across the floor. She twirled and spun back into center position, finishing with a pirouette. She could feel her smile broadening with every move; she felt the music carry her right up to her final curtsy.

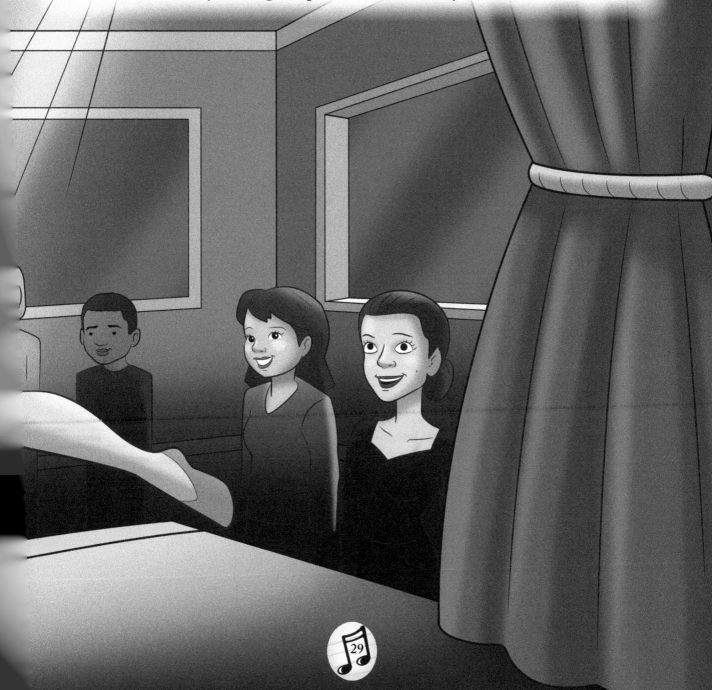

Her dance lasted just under two minutes, and her audition piece was done. Jensine quickly recovered her music and went out into the adjoining room of the studio.

There were a number of students waiting in the wings, just outside the makeshift stage. "That was astounding … wonderful … beautiful …," were some of the remarks she heard.

"Where on earth did you learn to dance like that?" someone asked. Jensine looked down at the CD, the sound of the song "Amazing Grace" still fresh in her mind. She paused, but only for a moment. Then her daddy's words came to her once more. "Let the music carry you," he often said, and she had done just that.

"I learned the steps from my dance teachers, but my daddy taught me to dance." She smiled as she and all of her friends began to laugh.

ABOUT THE AUTHOR

Susie Rich was raised in Cincinnati, Ohio, and has spent her career working in the social work/homelessness prevention field. Several years ago, she began to pursue her passion for writing; she has published "Beauties, The Eye of the Beholder," in an Ohio magazine. She has also written a number of short stories and is currently working on a novel. She resides near Boston, Massachusetts, with her husband, Douglas.

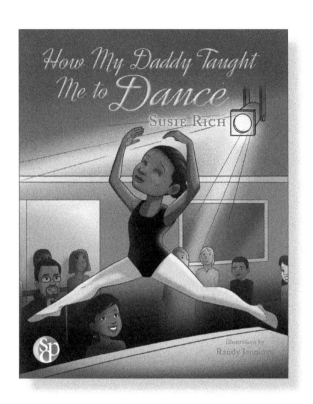

Hey kids! Did you love *How My Daddy Taught Me to Dance?*
Then read *Too Much Hopscotch,* also by Susie Rich.

HOW MY DADDY TAUGHT ME TO DANCE

SUSIE RICH

Children's book, ages 4-8

Author Website: www.SusiesStories.com

Publisher: SDP Publishing

Also available in ebook format

TO PURCHASE:
Amazon.com
BarnesAndNoble.com
SDPPublishing.com

SDP Publishing

www.SDPPublishing.com

Contact us at: info@SDPPublishing.com

CPSIA information can be obtained
at www.ICGtesting.com
Printed in the USA
BVHW021508280122
627226BV00003B/28